Dear Parents and Educators,

Welcome to Penguin Young Readers! As parents and educators, you know that each child develops at his or her own pace—in terms of speech, critical thinking, and, of course, reading. Penguin Young Readers recognizes this fact. As a result, each Penguin Young Readers book is assigned a traditional easy-to-read level (1–4) as well as a Guided Reading Level (A–P). Both of these systems will help you choose the right book for your child. Please refer to the back of each book for specific leveling information. Penguin Young Readers features esteemed authors and illustrators, stories about favorite characters, fascinating nonfiction, and more!

Fox on the Job

LEVEL **3**

GUIDED
READING
LEVEL **J**

This book is perfect for a **Transitional Reader** who:
- can read multisyllable and compound words;
- can read words with prefixes and suffixes;
- is able to identify story elements (beginning, middle, end, plot, setting, characters, problem, solution); and
- can understand different points of view.

Here are some **activities** you can do during and after reading this book:
- List all the words in the story that have an -ed ending. On a separate sheet of paper, write the root word next to the word with the -ed ending, using the chart below as an example.

word with -ed ending	root word
saved	save
showed	show

- Character Traits: Fox is honest. By telling the truth, Fox gets in trouble. Discuss how. What would you do if you were in Fox's situations?

Remember, sharing the love of reading with a child is the best gift you can give!

—Bonnie Bader, EdM
  Penguin Young Readers program

*Penguin Young Readers are leveled by independent reviewers applying the standards developed by Irene Fountas and Gay Su Pinnell in *Matching Books to Readers: Using Leveled Books in Guided Reading*, Heinemann, 1999.

For Clark Henley

Penguin Young Readers
Published by the Penguin Group
Penguin Group (USA) Inc., 375 Hudson Street, New York, New York 10014, USA
Penguin Group (Canada), 90 Eglinton Avenue East, Suite 700, Toronto, Ontario M4P 2Y3, Canada
(a division of Pearson Penguin Canada Inc.)
Penguin Books Ltd., 80 Strand, London WC2R 0RL, England
Penguin Group Ireland, 25 St. Stephen's Green, Dublin 2, Ireland (a division of Penguin Books Ltd.)
Penguin Group (Australia), 250 Camberwell Road, Camberwell, Victoria 3124, Australia
(a division of Pearson Australia Group Pty. Ltd.)
Penguin Books India Pvt. Ltd., 11 Community Centre, Panchsheel Park, New Delhi—110 017, India
Penguin Group (NZ), 67 Apollo Drive, Rosedale, Auckland 0632, New Zealand
(a division of Pearson New Zealand Ltd.)
Penguin Books (South Africa) (Pty.) Ltd., 24 Sturdee Avenue,
Rosebank, Johannesburg 2196, South Africa

Penguin Books Ltd., Registered Offices: 80 Strand, London WC2R 0RL, England

The Library of Congress has catalogued the Dial edition
under the following Control Number: 87015589

ISBN 978-0-14-037602-9   10 9 8 7 6 5 4 3 2 1

FOX ON THE JOB

by James Marshall

Penguin Young Readers
An Imprint of Penguin Group (USA) Inc.

Fox liked to show off
for the girls.
"Oh my!" said the girls.

One day Fox showed off just
a little too much.

"Look out!" cried the girls.

"Look out!"

Fox was saved,
but his bike
was a wreck.
"That's all right,"
he told the girls.
"I'll just ask my mother
for a new one."

"Now, see here, Fox," said Mom.

"I'm not made of money.

You will just have to get a job

if you want a new bike."

"A job!" said Fox.

"There must be some other way."

And he went to his little sister.

"Louise, dear," said Fox.

But Louise would not help.

"I'll scream!" she said.

"I won't forget this,"
said Fox.

"Who needs a bike, anyway?"

said Fox.

Just then Carmen rode by.

"Tra-la!" sang Carmen.

"That does it!" said Fox.

And he went to look for a job.

NEW SHOES

Downtown, Fox saw a sign

in a window.

HELP WANTED! NOW!

"I'm in luck," said Fox.

He went inside.

"Help is here!" he said.

"Not so fast," said the owner.

"Can you sell shoes?"

"Of course I can," said Fox.

"Are you honest?" said the owner.

"Oh yes!" said Fox.

"Well," said the owner.

"Let's give it a try.

You can start right away."

And he went to eat his lunch.

Fox kept himself busy.

"What an easy job," he said.

"Excuse me," said a lady.

"Can you help me?"

"That's what I'm here for,"

said Fox.

"I need some shoes,"

said the lady.

"Some pretty, little, pink ones."

Fox looked at the lady's feet.

"You can't mean it," he said.

"We may not *have* shoes that big.

Those are the biggest feet!"

"Well, I *never*!" cried the lady.

"What seems to be the trouble?"

said the owner.

"He said I have big feet!"

cried the lady.

"There, there," said the owner.

"Your feet are tiny."

And he turned to Fox.

"This is not the job for you."

"Well, I *never*!" said Fox.

THE
HAUNTED
HOUSE

Fox walked by

the amusement park.

"Too bad I don't have money

for a few rides," he said.

"I heard that," said Mr. Jones,

who ran the park.

"Perhaps you would like a job?"

"You don't mean it!"

said Fox.

Mr. Jones put Fox to work
at the Haunted House.

"What's inside?" said Fox.

"Oh, it's very scary,"
said Mr. Jones.

Fox's first customers were Carmen
and her little brother Clark.

"A ticket for the kid," said Carmen.

"Aren't you going in?" asked Fox.

"It's not scary enough," said
Carmen.

Fox and Carmen waited and waited.

"What's taking that kid so long?"
said Fox.
"Maybe he got lost," said Carmen.
"Why don't you go inside
and look for him?"

"I beg your pardon?" said Fox.

"You aren't scared, are you?"

said Carmen.

"Me, scared?" said Fox.

And he went into the

Haunted House.

Inside it was really something.

"Welcome to the Haunted House!"
cried a skeleton.

"I'm coming to get you!"
cried a ghost.

"Boo!" cried a vampire.

Poor Fox was as white as a sheet.

"Hi, Fox!" said Clark.

"I'll show you how to get out."

"For shame!" said Fox to Mr. Jones.

"That's no place for little kids!

I quit!"

"Oh, pooh," said Mr. Jones.

"They love it!"

PIZZA
TIME

Fox saw his friend Dexter
coming out of the pizza parlor.
"You can't fire *me*," said Dexter.
"I quit!"
"Fine," said the boss.
"Maybe my next delivery boy
won't eat up all the pizza!"
Dexter left in a huff.
And Fox stepped inside
the pizza parlor.

"Do you have a job for me?"
asked Fox.

"Do you like pizza?" said the boss.

"I prefer hot dogs," said Fox.

"Excellent," said the boss.

"Are you fast on your feet?"

"Like the wind," said Fox.

"Excellent," said the boss.

"Take this pizza over to

Mrs. O'Hara.

She has been waiting a long time."

Fox was out the door in a flash.

On Homer's Hill

Fox picked up speed.

"I'm the fastest fox in town,"

he said.

At that moment Louise came

around the corner.

She was taking her pet mice

to the vet for their shots.

It was quite a crash!

Fox, Louise, and everything else

went flying.

They saw stars.

"Now you've done it!" said Fox.

"You've made me late.

I'll really have to step on it!"

And he hurried away.

Louise went to the vet's.

Doctor Jane opened the box.

"Where are your pet mice?"

she said.

"This looks like a pizza."

"Uh-oh," said Louise.

Fox knocked on Mrs. O'Hara's door.

"It's about time," said Mrs. O'Hara.

"I'm having a party.

And we're just dying for pizza."

"It will be worth the wait," said Fox.

"Pizza time!" said Mrs. O'Hara
to her friends.
She opened the box.

Back at the pizza parlor

the boss was hopping mad.

"Mrs. O'Hara just called," he said.

"And you are fired!"

"Didn't she like the pizza?" said Fox.

A BRIGHT IDEA

"This just isn't my day," said Fox.

"But I'm not giving up.

I'll think of something."

Just then he came to

a furniture store.

And suddenly he had a bright idea.

"Business is bad, Fox,"
said the owner of the store.
"I can't give you a job."

"Maybe you can," said Fox.
And he told the owner his
bright idea.

Later that day Carmen and Dexter
were out for a stroll.

"Look at that," said Dexter.

A large crowd was standing
in front of the furniture store.

"I can't see," said Carmen.

"Lift me up."

Dexter lifted Carmen above
the crowd.

"What is going on?" said Dexter.

"It's Fox!" shouted Carmen.

"What a great bed!" said someone.

"I want one!" said someone else.

"What a great idea!" said the boss.

But Fox was already sound asleep—

and dreaming of his new bike.

E MARSH   FLT
Marshall, James
Fox on the job /

12/13